DIAMOND IN THE ROUGH

BOOK ONE

CORPER SHUN!!!

ADEBOLA A. AYOADE

SYNCTERFACE

Syncterface Media
London
www.syncterfacemedia.com

DIAMOND IN THE ROUGH: CORPER SHUN!!!

ISBN: 978-0-9933860-0-8
Copyright © January 2016 by Adebola A. Ayoade
All Rights Reserved

Published in the United Kingdom by

Syncterface Media
London

www.syncterfacemedia.com
info@syncterfacemedia.com

Cover Design by Syncterface Media

Appreciation

A BIG THANK YOU TO MY FAMILY AND ALL WHO MADE
THIS DREAM A REALITY

Contents

Prologue

It was 6pm on Monday, August 3rd. Mr & Mrs Aina had just left my office. It had been a long day and we had discussed extensively about their daughter whom according to them was becoming rebellious. They had wondered where they went wrong and why their daughter had turned out the way she did.

"She is our only child," Mr Aina said with a deep sigh.

"We sent her to the best schools, we sent her abroad for summer holidays, we got a private lesson teacher for her and gave her the best education you could ever think of," He continued.

"We bought her the best clothes, jewellery and every other accessory she requested for. There was nothing she asked for that we did not give her. In spite of everything we have done for her, she still claims we don't love her, we cage her and that she wants to be free," Mrs Aina added

I smiled at the word *free*. It sounded very familiar. "How old is she?" I asked.

"19 years, she will be 20 at the end of this year," Mrs Aina replied. That also sounded familiar, so I smiled again.

I watched the couple that sat opposite me with keen interest and I saw their countenance fall like the sunny day that suddenly turned cloudy. They were obviously disappointed. This couple reminded me of a couple I've known all my life. The whole scenario felt like I had seen it before.

"Please help us ma, we have heard so much about you and how you've helped transform the lives of young girls. We know you can help our daughter." Mrs. Aina pleaded.

"Hmm, what's her name?" I asked.

"Idunnu" Mrs Aina replied. All the while, Mr. Aina had been quiet.

"Could she come and see me?" I asked.

"That's the point, she has refused to see anyone," Mr Aina finally spoke up.

"Ok, could you give me her telephone number or her email address?" I asked.

"I could start up communication with her without her seeing me," I said.

"We will be grateful ma," Mrs Aina said with a sigh

of relief as she gave Idunnu's contact details.

"Thank you very much sir and ma, I'll get in touch with her," I said as I collected the contact.

"No, we should thank you for your help ma," Mrs Aina replied promptly.

"It's ok and you are welcome," I replied with a smile.

Idunnu was said to have been of good behaviour until her last days in the University when she suddenly started searching for freedom. Her quest for freedom had gone so wild that it had become a nightmare for her parents. Her parents complained about her incessant attendance at parties and her new habit of smoking and drinking.

At first, they thought she joined bad company but they realized she was the bad company as she was the leader of her gang. One of the days, when her parents confronted her, she was said to have called them failures and accused them of not caring about her and not been there when she needed them. She had promised to kill herself if she was questioned again about her lifestyle. The day she said that was the day her parents started searching for help. They had seen one of my conferences on TV and written out the contact address. That was how they found me.

After Mr & Mrs Aina left my office that evening, I sat back in my chair and reflected on the story they had told me about their daughter - Idunnu earlier that day. It had happened before and the outcome was predictable. I only hoped I was able to get through to Idunnu and get her to see me. I felt a sense of urgency to save the young girl, she may not get a second chance like a few of us did. I sank into my chair and gave a deep sigh.

"If only I knew better," I thought aloud.

<u>1</u>

How It All Began

It was a beautiful Tuesday. The cool breeze blew through my curtains with soothing sensation. It ran smoothly through my velvety skin in the most tender way and I felt I was gently carried by the steady calm waves of a flowing river in the mild darkness of the dawning of a new day.

"Knock! Its 4:30, wake up and start getting prepared so you won't miss your flight," My father's voice called outside my room when he knocked. He had his own unique way of knocking.

This hard knock had interrupted my beautiful sleep as I was just beginning to enjoy my journey to famous dreamland. Slowly, I dragged myself up from the bed like a snail dragging its shell on a long trip. I was very drowsy and I yawned severally like a few days old baby getting used to its new environment. It was obvious I needed to sleep a little more.

As I sat up and looked at the time, it was 4:35am and I smiled. It was October 15, the long awaited day. My flight was 6:50am and my house to the airport was less than an hour but for the traffic that usually made it longer. Check-in time closed at 6:30am, therefore, I had to be at the airport and be ready to fly before 6:20am. I had barely slept 20 mins before my father woke me. I wished I slept longer than that but I had to wake up. The Jos cold was just too sweet for me to be awake that early.

My name is Aderinmola Adeyosola. I'm close to my mid – thirties and I'm the only child of my parents. I am 5ft 3inches tall, fair in complexion with a perfect figure 8 shape. I'm friendly, playful and wild in my imagination. To a large extent, I'm adventurous in a quiet way. Generally, I'm reserved, I could be quiet but I'm gentle. The story I'm about to share with you happened a few years back when I was quite young and naive.

It all began in 2002. I had been numbering my days since 8th October when I went to school to collect my call-up letter for my NYSC, a national youth service program in Nigeria.

"WOW! Finally, I am going to serve," I whispered to myself in my sleepy voice. Since graduation in July, it had felt like years staying at home. The two months had felt like ten years! I had a lot of catching up to do in the area of domestic work at home and my mother was readily available to ensure I caught up.

Four years in the University away from home was enough to make me domestically lazy. Even during holidays, I had one thing or the other to do, one training or the other to go for. I never really stayed at home with my parents. When I finally graduated, I wanted to continue the tradition but my mother said "NO!" It was then I realised that my days of truancy were over and I had to learn how to be a good home maker. I had no choice but to obey.

2

Back To School

How can I forget that bright and sunny morning when I left my aunty's house to report at school to collect my call up letter? I had left Jos on Sunday evening to join the night bus to Lagos where I alighted at Ile-Ife early Monday morning where my aunt lived.

On my way to Ife, I thought about many things I'd like to do when I go for my NYSC, I fantasized about Lagos and wished desperately to be posted to Lagos. If I had my way, I would have worked my way to be posted but I knew no one so I just hoped for the best. The main thing was for me to be posted out of Jos, out of the comfort of my home and the watchful eyes of my parents. I was so engrossed in my thought that I did not realise there was a young man beside me who tried to chat me up until he tapped me.

"Hi, my name is Timi, you seem so lost thinking about something nice cause you've been smiling at yourself," He said like he had rehearsed his speech.

In my mind, I scoffed at him wondering how my personal fantasy was his business, but outwardly, I tried to be nice.

"Yea, I was just thinking happy thoughts that's all," I responded.

"What did you say your name was again?" He asked.

"I have not mentioned my name to you yet," I replied.

He laughed and said, "that was just a joke, I know. So tell me what's your name," He asked.

"I'm Derin," I replied sharply. I was already getting impatient with him because he interrupted my thoughts and it did not seem like he was going to stop anytime soon.

"I'm an artist, I basically draw and paint." He paused and continued, "you are pretty and I could do a painting of you if you would let me," He said with a smile.

I thought that was nice of him but I was not in the mood for a conversation and I was thinking hard on how to cut off the conversation.

"So what do you do Derin?" He asked.

"I'm a graduate about to go and serve, I'm just going to pick up my letter from school," I answered.

"Oh, Nice, Congrats! However, I don't mean to sound negative but I really do not fancy this NYSC stuff because one is back to square one after service," He said. At this point, I was determined to stop him.

"For instance, I became an Artist because I searched for a job for two years after NYSC. I was not retained at my place of primary assignment, so after two years of desperate search for a worthy employment, I started using my gift and here I am but..." He went on and on and I just tuned off. Eventually, I had to stop him.

"Ok, I get, experiences differ and I quite appreciate your story but if you don't mind, I'd like to be left alone. Thank you," I said bluntly.

"Oh, sorry, my apologies," He said and sat back into his chair like a just scolded 6 year old boy.

"No worries," I responded dismissively and continued with my fantasy as the journey continued. In no time, I dozed off only to wake up when the bus stopped at the garage at 5am.

I arrived at my Aunty's place at 6am as her house was just an hour from the garage. She was happy to see me, we talked all through the day and I went to bed early because I had to be in school on Tuesday morning. She was one of my mother's sisters. Her house was close to school so my parents asked me to stay over at her place since I would be at school on Tuesday.

I got to school quite early that morning and there were few students around. Distribution of call up letters to alumni was not going to start until 9am and I was already in school at 7:30am. I met some of my friends, immediate set after me and some acquaintances too. They were already in their final year and planning for their various projects.

"Once upon a time, I was like this," I smiled and I thought to myself. I went into the College Building to sit down. I picked out one of my books to read while I waited. Once it was 9am, the lecturers in charge walked into the College Building. I gave them 15 – 30 mins to settle at the venue for collection which was the second floor. After 30 mins, I went upstairs and I was among the first ten to collect their letters. By this time, students had started trooping in succession.

3

When Freedom Walked In

To my utter amazement, I was posted to Lagos and I was quite excited about that. It was a dream come true, I felt Heaven had smiled on me and I had been granted the freedom I craved for. As I walked through the College Building and fantasized about my 'would – be' adventure in Lagos, I suddenly came back to reality no thanks to the abrupt interruption.

"Derin baby!" My former roommate called out in excitement,

"Hey Annabel! How are you? Good to see you again roomey!" I responded in same manner as we hugged each other.

"Where were you posted?" I asked eagerly.

"Zamfara!" She said happily.

"You don't say?! Sharia State?" I asked in

amazement.

"Yes dear but don't worry, I will survive," She answered in her usual assuring tone.

"Yeah baby!" I responded, as we gave each other a high five.

"And you? Where were you posted?" She poked me.

"Lagos o, my dear," I answered.

"Really? The 'No man's' city!" She exclaimed happily for me.

"Yeah, I'm really going to explore mehn!" I answered back with my mischievous look.

"This girl ehn! Na God go help you, no go turn bad girl there o! You that have been looking for an excuse to go far away from home," She teased as she warned me not to go misbehave in Lagos.

Annabel knew I had always wanted to leave my parents to explore, she also knew my wild tendencies.

"Omo! Jos don tire me! Finally, I will be out of my parents' over protection! Derin, beware of bad boys o! Derin there are kidnappers around o! Derin this, Derin that, Derin, Deriin De-rin! At least, now, I'll just be a phone call a-waaayyy...," I said as I laughed and waved my phone at Annabel's face.

"Hmmmm! Derin, just be careful sha..." Annabel responded but I had to cut her off before she went preachy on me. Annabel could be a mother hen at times.

"Thank you Annabel," Just then, I spotted Annabel's Michael Kors Purse. It looked new and recently acquired. "Wow! Babe, no be MK be that?" I asked and gave her my curious look.

"Na da, I'm not giving you this one, you will strip me of all my designers o," Annabel said no and shook her head vehemently.

"Haba, chill na, wait o, is that not Sean?" I asked pretending to see Annabel's boyfriend. As Annabel turned to see if it was her boyfriend, I snatched the purse and ran away. "Hey, Derin, lai lai, not this one," She said as she ran after me as I laughed and ran into the College Building.

As I ran into the College Building, I bumped into the college officer, Mr. Gbolahan. Mr. Gbolahan was popularly known and called Mr. Gb. He was a tall, dark and handsome man with an admirable charisma. He smiled always and had a very attractive aura. He was a very friendly man who wanted everyone around him to be happy. He was also the first after Annabel to know when I was going to have a relationship with Shaye and he was glad that I was going to date someone he knew quite well and could vouch for.

Shaye was my boyfriend in school. We were very fond of each other. Mr. Gb had known Shaye when Shaye was in secondary school but he knew me when I was a Jambite (*a nick name given to newly registered students in the University*) during registration and we became friends over the years. He was single so people actually thought we had something not knowing he took me more like a younger sister he never had. The day he asked about my relationship life and I told him about Shaye and my intention to date him, he was very glad. He told me Shaye was his younger brother from another mother and he was glad to have me as an in-law peradventure Shaye and I got married someday.

"Boom!" I hit the table to avoid colliding with Mr. Gb.

"Whoa Derin, you've started your rough play again, at your old age," He said,

"Haba, Mr. Gb, na wa for you o, sorry I almost bumped into you, Bel was running after me" I said with a smile and my usual patronising way.

Then I whispered "I snatched her MK purse. She just bought it, you know my usual way na" I said with a wink. Annabel's name was usually interchanged with either Anna or Bel.

Mr. Gb only laughed and shook his head, then he said "Anyway, congrats on your posting, I saw Lagos, but Shaye was posted to PH o, PortHarcourt, I hope you know? And I hope you won't miss him too much?" He said with a little mischief in his smile.

With mixed feelings, I answered "wow, that's far!"

"Of course, I will miss him," I said in a low tone but almost immediately I said "but we'll definitely work something out."

Just then Annabel caught up with me and tried to get her MK purse from me, I immediately hid behind Mr. Gbolahan, we both giggled, then she looked at me, gave a surrender sigh as she shook her head.

"There is nothing I can do about you Derin, you can have the purse, just give me my money and my documents inside," She said.

"Good afternoon Mr. Gb! How are you today sir?" Annabel greeted Mr. Gbolahan after she gave up her chase on me.

"I'm fine Annabel and you?" He asked.

"I'm fine too sir, just this bully called Derin that has stripped me of all my designers!" She answered pointing at me accusingly.

"That's why she's your roommate and best friend," He said and laughed.

"Abi o," I responded with my tongue out.

As if he remembered something Mr. Gbolahan said to us "I have to leave now, you girls have fun ok? And Derin, stop being naughty, regards to Shaye, Anna, regards to Sean"

"Yes sir," we chorused.

When he left, I told Annabel what Mr. Gb said. She looked worried too but I assured her that Shaye and I would be fine. Annabel was worried about Shaye and I because we were too close and inseparable in school. She knew what we went through and how strong we had been together. She would be hurt if we broke up.

PortHarcourt is located in the South-South part of Nigeria. It is the Capital of Rivers State, one of the oil producing states in Nigeria. PortHarcourt is usually called PH for short and it is known for its good, bad and ugly stories just like any and every other place in the world. Annabel was a little skeptical about Shaye's posting to PortHarcourt. She was more worried about some of the young girls there who were ready to pounce on any good looking man they desired.

While we were chatting away, someone covered my eyes from behind me. I knew those palms, those strong, firm smooth palms that were so masculine. With a smile on my face, I said

"Shaye love, I know you are the one, quit the suspense and hug me now sweets," He removed his hands and tickled me a little, we laughed, played and hugged each other, just then Anna coughed

"Ahem, I'm still here o," She teased.

"Oh sorry, Hi babes," Shaye greeted Anna while he still held my hand.

"Hello Shaye, happy reunion," She teased again as she referred to our previous drama.

"Thanks," Shaye laughed. "Collected your letter yet?" He asked.

"Yes, I have," replied Annabel.

"Baby, have you? I just came in, we could go in together if you haven't," He said as he swung me gently in a rhythmic way.

I told him I had collected mine but I would not tell him where I was posted until he collected and told me his. I did not let him know what Mr. Gbolahan already told me. Just then, Annabel's phone rang, she excused herself to receive the call.

When Annabel excused herself to pick her call, Shaye suggested we waited for her to finish before we proceeded to collect his letter. It was a good idea and I agreed. So we found a corner at the reception of the College Building where I almost collided with Mr. Gb to sit down. It was obvious we had missed each other so much. I could not let him know my house yet, so we spent bulk part of the holiday talking on phone.

The first time we saw after graduation was in September when the Alumni had a brief meeting for fresh graduates (which was our set). It was a two day meeting to officially welcome us into the Alumni Association. I told my parents it was a four day meeting because I wanted to spend more time with Shaye. My aim was to spend the third day with Shaye and rest the fourth day before leaving the fifth day for Jos. I stayed with my Aunty for those five days. She knew how my parents could be and also understood my need for mingle as an only child. She was strict and principled yet she was flexible. It was easier for me to tell her the truth than it was for me to tell my parents. They must not know I had a boyfriend talk less of bringing him home. My Aunty always warned me to be careful and never supported me sleeping over at Shaye's place which was also at Ile-Ife. She adviced me when the opportunity availed itself and she scolded me when I needed it.

The second time was that day we went for our call up letters. We sat so close to each other and I looked into his eyes with rapt attention as he told me about his holiday.

In the course of the conversation, Shaye asked to ease himself. I watched him leave and as he walked away, I stared at him with a smile on my face as I thought to myself how far we had come.

4

Love At First Sight?

I remember when Shaye and I first met. I was a Broadcast/Journalism Student, Department of Mass Communication, Communication of Language Arts in the College of Arts and Humanities in 200 level. It was a sunny Saturday afternoon at the Obafemi Awolowo University Library, Ile-Ife, Osun State, Nigeria.

Annabel and I had left the hostel that morning to start our News Writing and Reporting Assignment. Annabel had teased me that I was off to the library for a blind date because I had taken my time to dress up. I wore a red fitted knee length dress with a classy yet casual Kenneth Cole pair of sandals. My cream fresh water pearl necklace sat gracefully on my neck; the pin ear rings with bracelets to match the sandals; and my swatch wrist watch made me look amazeballs. I had relaxed my hair in the middle of the week, so I styled it on this fateful Saturday and put a red rose pin ribbon to hold it a little to the side to give it the Barbie feel. I also took my time to apply my make-up to match my dressing and we were almost late for the time we planned to arrive at the Library. It was not like I expected to meet any one that day, I just felt I should give myself a little treat. When I finished, we stepped out briskly.

As we walked to the library with the University Campus busy with students both old and new, I couldn't help but notice how some male students stole glances at me and gave out cat calls but Annabel and I ignored them. We laughed at them and Annabel teased me that I was the cause of the attention.

The library was a two-storey building with the ground floor for group discussions and students meeting point, the first floor for Sciences and the second floor for Arts and Humanities. Many students sat at different parts on the ground floor. Some had their group discussions, some chatted away, some made calls quietly, while some browsed the internet. There were clusters of girls and boys, new students popularly called Jambites, as well as old students popularly called sophomores.

I went straight to the Broadcast/Journalism section on the second floor to pick a book on News Writing and Reporting. I finally found one, opened it to glance through and was carried away reading a particular chapter when I was interrupted by a deep calm voice.

"Hello, please do you know a book titled Introduction to Mass Communication by err..," He scratched his head to remember.

"Bittner," I completed it for him.

"Ah yes," he agreed with a smile. "Thank you," He said.

Immediately, I fell into the beautiful world of fantasy. He was a tall, fair and handsome guy, he had lovely brown piercing eyes, his smile exposed his perfectly arranged white teeth, with a pencil lined gap tooth that rested gently on his lower pink lip. I was carried away in split seconds and jolted back to reality.

"Excuse me!" Shaye said and waved his hand across my face to get my attention.

"Oh Sorry, ah, yes, yes, Bittner right?" I flushed with embarrassment.

"It's alright," he smiled again. "Yes, Bittner," he responded.

Immediately, I got myself together and helped him get the book.

As I searched for the book, I noticed he took a quick look at me a few times and I thought to myself "does he like me?" My heart raced like the leaps of a kangaroo, my eyes sparkled like the twinkle of a new star, I was as restless as a man whose wife was in labour of their first child but I quickly composed myself. I went to the other side of the shelf to check for the book and seized the opportunity to steal quick glances at him too.

He had a well-built body and my heart melted when he ran his fingers through his black curly hair. I knew there and then I was attracted to him. I immediately found the book and went back to him.

"There you are," I said as I gave him. "It's actually titled the other way round, Mass Communication, An

Introduction," I completed my statement with a smile.

"Oh, thank you," He said and nodded in agreement as he flipped through the pages of the book.

"You are welcome," I replied.

Then he looked at me and said "Nice dress."

"Oh thank you," I replied with a composed smile but I almost exploded inside.

"By the way, my name is Shaye, Folashaye Origbade," he stretched his right hand to shake my hand.

"Pleased to meet you Shaye, I'm Derin, Aderinmola Adeyosola," as I received his handshake.

His palm, was strong, firm and smooth. It felt so masculine against my soft, feminine and tender palm. I immediately removed my hand so as not to drift again. I looked around the library, a little nervously to see if no one saw us. I saw that no one was looking, then I sighed quietly.

"Are you a Jambite?" I asked to ease the nervous feeling that was building inside me.

He looked at me and smiled "Nopes, I'm in 200 level," He answered.

"Really? How come we've not met till now?" I asked. "I'm also in 200 level," I said surprised but jumping happily inside me.

"Wow! That's great, I guess we haven't met because I'm in the College of Science and Technology, I'm a Mechanical Engineering Student," He answered again with a smile.

I was surprised and happy at the same time, so I probed further to find out why he was in the Arts and Humanities section of the library and specifically Broadcast/Journalism to pick a communications book. He said he was in that section of the library that day because he came to get a book for his younger sister who was also a Mass Communications student but in 100 level. He said a friend recommended that particular book for his sister who had a little difficulty with one of her assignments. At this time, I had started to relax and get more comfortable speaking with him.

While we talked in the library, I noticed Shaye's gentle manly nature. I thought he was of mixed race but to my surprise, he had never boarded a plane to travel within the country not to mention travelling abroad or be born there. Both his parents were full Nigerians but his paternal grand dad was a citizen of United States of America.

Shaye's paternal grandfather had visited Nigeria many years ago to start a company. In the course of his work, he met Shaye's paternal grandmother and employed her. She was quite hard working and diligent too. Shaye's grandfather had observed her closely and became attracted to her over time. After a year of diligently working for him, he proposed to Shaye's grandmother, married her and had Shaye's father who was the only child. When Shaye's Father graduated from the University, his father informed him of plans to return to the USA. This did not please Shaye's Father. He chose to remain in Nigeria to continue Shaye's grandfather's business. Five years after Shaye's grandparents left Nigeria, Shaye's Father met Shaye's mother and married her. They had only two children, Shaye and his sister. One day, when Shaye and his sister were little, Shaye's father was involved in a car accident where he died on the spot. The shock of the news made Shaye's mother a vegetable which made caring for her children a challenge so for close to fifteen years, they lived with their maternal grandmother and, at times, had to fend for themselves.

Shaye's Father's original surname was Macaulay, he was Mr. Origbade Macaulay. According to Shaye, he preferred to use his father's first name to maintain his root, hence Folashaye Origbade.

I liked Shaye immediately I saw him. I told myself, he could only have existed in my fantasy world. We chatted for a long time and forgot we were in the library. He was funny and he had a way of passing compliments passively.

"Excuse me please, could you lower your voices. This is the 'Silent Zone', otherwise you may want to go to the ground floor," The Librarian said quietly but firmly.

She was a young dark complexioned woman probably in her thirties. She was single, quite strict and could be mean at times but when it came to the academic progress of any student, she could go the extra mile. From other students' reports, she disliked relationships, so once she saw a male and female together she tried to separate them. Her real name was Miss Shamptey but she was nicknamed 'Miss No Pairing' by students.

"Oh, we are sorry, we got carried away," Shaye replied the attendant.

I looked around and saw some angry faces. some students stared at us with a mischievous smile, some just shook their heads and continued to read, while others ignored us and remained buried in their books. I felt embarrassed but I had to cover up. I did not realise we created so much attention. At that point, Anna found me.

"Babe, I've been waiting for you. Where's the book?" She whispered. Anna, most times, called me babe or any other pet name but also called me, Derin, occasionally.

"Here," I gave it to her. "Sorry, I got caught up in a conversation, Miss No Pairing just corrected us. Meet Shaye, I just met him," I whispered back quickly.

Anna and Shaye exchanged pleasantries quickly and in a whisper. This time, the Librarian cleared her throat and gave me a warning look. I waved her an apology and whispered to Annabel indicating we needed to leave.

As I turned to leave, Shaye held my wrist and whispered "I'll like to see you again."

5

I'm In Love!

The butterflies in my stomach flew around rapidly, I just had to act really composed outside. "I'll be on the ground floor with Anna till 6pm," I whispered back. It was 3pm then.

"Ok, see you 6pm," He whispered again with a smile.

Anna and I immediately rushed out, though quietly downstairs to start our assignments. I felt a few eyes following us but did not bother to look around to avoid further embarrassment.

We arrived at the ground floor as quickly as possible, Annabel already picked a space for us at the corner of the room where some of our course mates were gathered too, so she led the way and we sat down. The number of students on the ground floor had increased within the space of an hour since we got there. I did not know I had spent much time on the first floor, no wonder Anna came upstairs to look for me, she must have wondered what happened to me.

For the next few minutes, I found it very difficult to focus; every thing Anna said to me those few minutes sounded like an echo. All I saw was Shaye's smile; all I heard while Anna spoke was Shaye's calm yet masculine voice; all I felt when Anna tapped me was Shaye's strong palm when he held my wrist when Anna and I were about to leave. All I saw was Shaye. Then, suddenly, I interrupted Annabel.

"Bel," I said, as I called her occasionally, "I think I'm in love," I said quietly looking her straight in the eyes.

I could see the shock written all over Annabel. Her eyes widened like they would pop out, her jaw dropped like she had seen a ghost and slowly she used the back of her hand to touch my neck to feel my temperature and said;

"Babe, you well so?" This meant "Babe, Are you well?"

"Do I look like I'm not well?" I asked giving her a serious look.

Anna spent some part of her life in the Niger Delta region which is South-South part of Nigeria, so she sometimes exhibited their characteristics, one of which is Pidgin English also known as broken English in Nigeria. This kind of English Language is not spoken like general English Language.

"Shuu? So o all d talk talk wey I don do, shin shin no enter your ear? Chai! My friend don miss road o," she said as she shook her head. This meant "So, you did not hear a single word from all I said? My friend has lost focus."

"Bel, to be honest, no! I didn't hear a single word. My mind has been on that guy," I answered with a serious countenance.

Annabel gave me a funny look to question if I was for real. She must have seen me in a different light that day.

"I'm serious, that guy took me off balance. I have not been able to focus since we came here," I said.

She wanted to laugh but when she looked at me again, she knew I was serious. She just smiled, held my hand and said

"Ok, I've heard you, we'll talk about it later tonight, for now, we have a News Writing and Reporting Assignment to complete, which is the main reason our parents sent us here, so, let's deal with that first. Ok?"

"Ok" I answered like a child. Then she responded sarcastically to tease me.

"My friend Derin is in love," she laughed but I ignored her and we continued with our work.

After much struggle, I finally succeeded in concentrating and we were able to do the assignment half way.

6

Her Coach, My Lover

Shaye met us at 6pm just as we were packing up our things to leave. At this time, more students were trooping in since the library opened for 24 hours. Most students came in at evening times even though some of them had other reasons for being there.

Shaye wanted to see us off to the hostel but I politely asked him not to. I did not know how I would have been able to compose myself beside him for a long time if I allowed him see us off, so I had to save myself the embarrassment. However, I offered to help his sister through with her assignment and he was grateful. I requested for his sister's room number which he released without hesitation and fortunately, his sister and I shared the same hostel. Shaye and I also exchanged phone numbers as we bade each other farewell that evening.

When Anna and I got to the hostel that evening, she

brought up the topic of Shaye and I which we put aside in the library earlier that day. I told her about all that transpired that afternoon as she listened with very rapt attention. She asked me lots of questions including why I thought I was already in love? If I knew if the feeling was mutual? If I was ready to date him and so on? She mentioned that it could merely have been an attraction or probably infatuation.

Bel explained to me that attraction was an emotion that caused an interest or desire in something or someone, which in my case, was someone. She said infatuation was also an emotion of unreasoned passion. Most people mistook it for love which could be what I was feeling for Shaye. Love, in my case, could have meant erotic love since all my description of him was about his physical attributes. She went further to remind me that infatuation was usually intense and short-lived and most times did more harm than good.

She said, even though physical attraction was necessary for a relationship, it should not be the focus, she told me to wait and first, be his friend, get to know him better and to see if a relationship with him was worth it. She also said I should allow him chase me. She emphasized that he was the man, so he should be the hunter. She warned that if I allowed my emotions override me and I chased him, I'll lose my dignity and respect as a lady and also kill the hunter in him. Besides, I would not be able to find out if the feeling was mutual. I was grateful for Annabel's advice. She had had a few relationships before me. Despite the fact that we were in 200 level together and she was my best friend, she was also five years older than I was.

Annabel had, twice, been denied admission into

two different Universities because she did not hit the cut off mark in the Joint Admission Matriculation Board Examination (JAMB), for her desired course which was International Relations.

JAMB was one of the required examinations candidates had to pass to gain admission into Federal or State Universities in Nigeria. When she finally passed her JAMB examination, at the third attempt, she was admitted into Obafemi Awolowo University. This time, she applied for Communication and Language Arts. We met on the first day of registration and bonded very fast. We respected each other and she knew how to switch personalty roles from sister to friend to aunty and more when the occasion demanded it. This time, she needed to advice me like an elder sister, because it was my first relationship and she wanted to see me happy.

The next day, which was a Sunday, I went to check for Shaye's sister in the afternoon. I met her, introduced myself and helped her with her assignment. She said Shaye had called and informed her earlier about me so she expected me and was glad I came. Her assignment was quite simple. All she needed was a little more explanation on what she was required to do which we did together. I could see the relief on her face after we were through. She looked much happier than when we started. She thanked me and asked me to stay a little longer for some entertainment. After much appeal, I obliged.

Shaye's sister was quite friendly and she seemed like a lively person. She asked me a few questions about myself, my studies and University life generally. She also shared her experiences as a Jambite in school.

From all she told me, she sounded excited about being in a University. She talked a little about how close she and her brother, Shaye were and how he could go to any length for her. She said her brother had never being in a relationship before because he wanted someone he was sure he would marry and the person had to be his sister's best friend. This information gave me an incline to the kind of person Shaye was. Shaye's sister didn't say so much but her little information was helpful. I listened attentively and kept the information safely in the corner of my heart. After staying with her for close to thirty minutes, I told her I was leaving. She was grateful I stayed and saw me off to the stairs. I went back to my room that evening happy and fulfilled.

When I got to the room, Annabel was already asleep, I looked at her with much admiration as I remembered our discussion the previous day. I moved closer to her, gave her a peck on the cheek and whispered "Rest well, sister I never had."

I went to bed happy with thoughts of Shaye, his sister's information and Annabel's words. I hoped for the best and looked forward to a better week. It was indeed a beautiful weekend.

On Monday afternoon, Shaye called to thank me for the assistance I gave his sister. He also talked about how his sister said a lot of good things about me from the few hours we spent together and officially made me his sister's personal coach. We became very good friends and his sister was very fond of me.

I took Annabel's advice seriously and Shaye was mature enough to build friendship with me. We talked on the phone, exchanged messages, agreed to meet a few times and overtime, he requested for my room number which I happily gave to him. He came to my hostel often, we ended up having common friends, ate together and did almost everything together. With time we became very fond of each other, Shaye finally asked me out, three months into our friendship and my answer was obviously a "Yes." Anna, Mr. Gb and Shaye's sister were happy for both of us.

7

Dream Come True

I gave a deep sigh as I came back from my long flash back. I almost forgot I was still in the College Building where Shaye had left me to go ease himself. Indeed, we had come a long way. From a harmless library meeting to helping his sister and there we were about to go and serve. I would definitely miss him.

"So, do you want to share the fantasy?" Shaye's voice whispered into my ears.

"Gasps," I held my breath... "Gosh! You scared me!" I said holding my chest.

"Awww, sorry love, I did not mean to, I saw you smiling all alone," He replied putting his hand across my neck.

"How long have you been here?" I asked. "errm, close to ten minutes," he replied.

"What?!!!" I exclaimed out of shock.

"Yea, I saw you staring into the air smiling and I did not want to interrupt your thoughts but when I saw the tears rolling down, I had to speak up," He answered.

"Oh, really?" I said as I wiped the tears off my eyes, "I did not even know I was crying," I said and laughed. I did not know the flash back I had had brought tears to my eyes, even though they were tears of joy.

At that time, the College Building had become quite busy with students who walked to and fro, some talked loudly while some became noisy from exclamations of joy from seeing one another again since graduation.

Shaye and I had to move to a less noisy place, close to the College Office, so we could talk. We picked our chairs and put it just beside the entrance of the office so Annabel would not have to look for us when she was done with her phone conversation. She was the reason we waited at the reception in the first place.

"So, what was it you were thinking about?" Shaye asked.

"Us, good things about us," I said quickly and before he could ask the obvious next question, I quickly interrupted, "Bel isn't through with her call yet? She has been gone for over fifteen minutes now. Right?" I asked checking my wrist watch.

Just then Annabel walked back, grinning from ear to ear, ready to pop out of her skin. "Alright guys I have to go now, Sean just called me that he is around. I'm sorry to have kept you waiting," She said trying hard not to run.

"Just ke? Bel, you've been gone for close to twenty minutes," I said with one of my eye brows raised. She understood what I said and in an attempt to avoid my tease, she said, "Derin don't start."

"Alright girl, take care and enjoy, call me later," I replied with a wink. She laughed because she understood the wink and said

"Ok dear!"

After she left, Shaye and I went upstairs where the call up letters were given. It was a large room and one of the largest in the department. For some reasons best known to the school authorities, they decided to merge the Sciences and Arts Students together to give them their letters. The population was large, the queue was long, people rushed, pushed one another, some fell and at some point, the scene became quite annoying. Somehow, Shaye and I managed to get in the queue.

There were three senior lecturers who sat behind a long table in the room that was used. One was from the College of Arts and Humanities who sat at the right hand side of the table, one was from the College of Business Administration who sat at the left hand side of the table and the middle one was the Dean of the College of Science and Technology who was the darkest in complexion of the three lecturers. He hardly ever smiled. He frowned so much that it was scary when he smiled. It was obvious he had his hair cut the previous day because there was no strand of hair on his head and his head shone like a new stainless steel pot. He called the names of Science and Technology students to hand over their call up letters to them.

The three lecturers had stern faces and they looked frustrated by the noise and disorderliness. Despite their frustration, they still called Students' names, even though, most times in anger. However, this hardly affected the students. The students continued in their ways.

As Shaye tried to get proper balance, he felt a slap on his back. In shock, he turned to see who it was and with great delight he shouted

"Hey Big man! How are you?" It was Ishaya, his very close class mate.

"Shaye da fine boy! I dey o, How you dey na?" Ishaya replied. Shaye always got praised for his good looks even from his male friends. He was that good looking.

"O boy fear catch me sha, I wan follow the person yarn say wetin I do?" Shaye said. This meant "I was scared, I was going to ask the person what I did wrong to deserve a slap on my back."

"Hahaha, upon your six packs you dey fear again, abeg joor, you suppose know say na only me fit do that kain tin na," Ishaya responded teasing Shaye that Shaye had no right to be scared because of his masculine body. He also reaffirmed that he, Ishaya was the only one bold enough to hit Shaye the way he did

They hugged each other like men do and they talked happily amidst the noise. "Madam! I hail o!" Ishaya turned to greet me with a salute. This was an informal way of saying "hello madam."

"Ish Ish, how now? Please don't scare us like that again o," I said with a smile. I called him Ish or Ish Ish as a short form for his name.

"No lele, no worries ma, apologies for scaring you, Shaye was my target," He said.

"No problem, it's ok," I replied.

Ishaya Folagbade, who I met through Shaye, was one of the best students in Computer Science. He was also a book worm and a walking computer but Ishaya was a little playful and he could be mischievous. One of his pranks was what he did to Shaye when he gave him a playful slap on his back, just to scare him and he achieved his aim.

"Folashaye Origbade," the Dean of Science and Technology called. Shaye walked up boldly to the front to collect his letter while Ishaya and I waited for him. When he came out, he had an indifferent look on his face, this time, Ishaya bade us farewell, so he could go collect his letter too. I did not like the indifference on his face, so I asked pretending to know nothing.

"So what's up? Where?" I asked acting curious.

"PH, PortHarcourt," He answered plainly.

"Cool!" I said with excitement. Then, concerned about his indifference, I asked

"Are you ok?"

"Sorry dear, I just have many issues on my mind." Then he lightened up and asked "So do you want to tell me where you were posted to now?"

In a playful way, I said, "guess"

"PH too," He winked.

"Ha ha ha, you wish! another trial," I said.

"Abuja?" he tried again. This time I laughed very hard and said "durrh! for the last time man!"

With an exasperated sigh, he replied "Ha! I give up, tell me and save me from this suspense"

"Ok! Lagos!" I answered smiling.

"What?! Why so far?" He asked, I could see the horror in his eyes.

Surprised at his reaction, I asked "and is there anything wrong with Lagos?"

"No dear, but...," He tried answering.

"But I'm happy! We could visit each other you know?" I interrupted.

"And we have few days to spend together before we part ways," I said softly.

"I'm sorry about my reaction Derin, just that I will miss you," He responded as he drew close to me.

"I'll miss you too Shaye I hope I don't cry," I responded.

"No baby you won't and in case you do, here's my shoulder, you can lean on me," we ended the statement together with the song and laughed again.

After the "drama" we left the College Building, At that time, afternoon was gradually slipping into evening and the number of students had reduced, as well as the noise and excited chatter. Shaye pulled me close to him and put his hand round my neck like he usually did when we walked together.

"Well! Well! Well! I'm hungry, may we go eat?" Shaye asked.

"Yes of course," I answered with delight. "It is an essential commodity," I added as we both walked down to the cafeteria. There was a little distance between the College Building and the cafeteria so we walked slowly with our hands held together as trees clapped to celebrate the cool breeze. The birds sang happily and the clouds flipped in slowly to usher in the evening time as the sun set.

8

Wandering Thoughts

As we walked down, my thoughts drifted. I was so excited with the feeling of going to serve in Lagos that I forgot my love was close to me. I imagined the adventure. I thought to myself.

"I am finally going to be let loose. The popular Lagos, I will be there, live and in concert! Hmmm, now I am going to know what and how it feels to be a bad girl."

As I smiled to myself quietly in response to my imagination, suddenly, I remembered Shaye.

"Hmm," I sighed.

"Am I still going to be faithful to him?" I asked myself.

"Will I still keep him?" I looked at him with a smile.

I'm sure he thought I smiled at what he said when, in honesty, I heard nothing.

"Do I really want to be tied to a relationship forever and not know what it means to date other guys? Party? Smoke? Drink? Sleep around?"

"I'm tired of being a virgin, this is my first relationship. Mum and Dad must not even know I'm dating anyone. I have been a good girl enough. Afterall, I graduated with a 2:1 GPA and the way these girls talk about sex, it sounds exciting and not harmful in the least." My thoughts wandered.

"This so called bad girls in school look happy and get the 'big dons'."

Big dons is an expression used in Nigeria for the rich, well known and respected personalities in the land.

"Look at Imeh," I continued with my thoughts "I heard she's getting married to the Governor's son before we go and serve, they already have a house, car and all the necessities of life waiting for them as soon as they are married. Look at Mariam, she is not even going to serve, the commissioner is sending her abroad for her masters. What about Dayo? the Permanent Secretary already set up a business for her and Ugo? Ugo rubs it in my face daily of how she allowed Deputy Comptroller disvirgin her and now after three weeks in camp she has straight employment into Customs Office. Shaye is just coming up, still living with his maternal grandmother sef. Me I want Olorunsogo, not Surulere." Olorunsogo and Surulere are native names in Yorubaland, the western part of Nigeria. Olorunsogo means 'God does glorious things', it is also an idiomatic expression for a comfortable or rich person while Surulere means 'Patience has its reward' and an idiomatic expression for a poor person or someone who is not financially successful yet.

As I thought along these lines, my heart shook. I wasn't even sure about Shaye, I wondered if he had thoughts similar to mine. He reminded me always of his commitment both in words and in deeds but then, I thought to myself

"Is it because we see each other in school almost everyday? What would happen when we leave the comfort zone of school for the NYSC camp?"

Then I remembered PortHarcourt girls. I've heard so much about those girls and their escapades. I thought to myself

"My Shaye, will he fall into their hands?"

As thoughts swam back and forth in my heart, I came back to my original thoughts and then another set of questions popped up

"Is there really joy in being a bad girl? Or are these girls just pretending?"

These and many other thoughts barraged my mind like an unleashed volcano. As an only child, I had been under the compulsory protection of my parents. In SS2, my father told me I was too young to have male friends. To this day, I still wish Nelson, my classmate back then, did not call the land line at the time he did. If only he had called a minute later, I would have been the one to pick that call and avoided getting into trouble. My mum watched my every step and always reminded me not to smile at boys as this only indicated that I was loose. Their love for me and protection of me were that strong. In as much as their counsel and training helped me in a tremendous way, a part of me felt loved and accepted while another part of me was stiff, paranoid and fearful.

I remembered when I started my menstrual cycle, mum told me, "don't let any boy touch you, once a boy touches you, you will get pregnant and that will mean bye-bye to your education." I took this advice lightly and secretly laughed at it because I knew her description of pregnancy wasn't quite as literal. The next day Dele, another classmate mistakenly hit my wrist when he almost fell in class during break time. I remembered how I was stricken with fear when I did not see my period the next month, I remembered how I beat myself about why I did not take my mother's words serious, how I should have told her Dele touched me, we probably could have found a solution early enough. But I was too scared to tell my parents anything. I only discovered later when I asked our school matron then, that I did not have my period that month because I had it twice the previous month which was the first time of my menstrual cycle.

Matron Bisi, as she was called, told me, since it was my first time ever, hormonal changes were expected, irregularities were also expected but not for long and with time, the body would adjust, which was so. It was Matron Bisi that taught me proper sex education and helped me understand the woman's anatomy. I fondly remembered her with a smile.

I knew they loved me so much, they gave me the best education, bought everything I wanted and needed that they deemed useful for me especially for my education. They took me out to places, we attended family parties together even though I was always under their watchful eyes. They took turns to drop me off at school themselves, picked me up when I closed from school. Sometimes, they dropped me off and picked me after school hours together. They were always parked outside just before school closed.

One day, a coincidence happened, as my mother and I drove out of the parking lot after school hours, my father was driving in to come pick me up, if he had come a minute after, he could have missed us. They both came from their different work places. We ended up going home together that day. They were that committed to me growing up.

As loving as they were, they were also conservative. They never discussed with me certain topics like sex education, dating relationships and other puberty or peer concerns because they felt I was still young and naïve. My movies were censored and I could only discuss limited and general things at home. I learnt more from asking questions and reading back then. These and a few other reasons made me feel caged in the house (even though I liked most parts of it) and I looked forward to freedom some day which finally came in the guise of NYSC.

My thoughts drifted again to my 'would-be' adventure and questions. Then finally I sighed and told myself "Well, I'll find out when I get there."

"Kai! Lagos na wa o, gaskiya fa, I'll finally go to that popular city called Lag!"

I heard my thoughts screaming inside me and I caught myself smiling again. I shrugged and said again to myself "being adventurous is not bad except when you take it to the extreme."

I was jolted back to reality when suddenly I felt a violent shake in my body.

"Derin!" Shaye said as he shook me.

Apparently, I had forgotten I was with him. He had poured out his heart, told me what he thought about when we were upstairs, but I did not hear a single word. I had been carried away in my world. He looked at me a little concerned and asked "What's the problem? Why are you smiling all alone? What I'm saying is not a joke is it?"

Disappointed in myself and apologetic at the same time, I said "I'm sorry Shaye, I did not know you were saying something."

"It's ok," Shaye responded in a low and disappointed tone. "It's probably not relevant now. You are still in the happy euphoria of Pre - NYSC."

I did not know what to say, I couldn't defend myself. Shaye was right. My God! I was so deep in thought that I had lost touch with reality and not heard a word Shaye said. I felt so terrible, I stopped walking and I stopped him too, I turned to him, looked into his brown piercing eyes and said again

"I'm sorry love, I got carried away, I am just excited about the whole thing and imagining what it would be like in another city."

Then I held him tenderly, "You know, having being born, bred and buttered in Jos, I am just excited that finally I will be away from my parents for a whole year.

I've heard so much about Lagos and going there now thrills me."

As if he saw something for the first time, Shaye looked at me wide eyed.

"So you mean you did not hear all I was saying?"

At this point, I became ashamed of myself, yet I answered honestly.

"To be honest with you dear, I did not."

Shaye's countenance dropped more, but I immediately said "Look, I'm sorry, really I am, ok I'm all ears now."

"Never mind," Shaye replied.

I was determined to get it over with, I never wanted to hurt Shaye, so as he walked forward I stood in front of him and said

"Ha ha now, but I said I am sorry, you know I'm a great listener, today is just different."

"Sweet? Talk to me, love," I pressed on.

Then I tickled him like we did to each other, at first, he tried to resist and then he gave in, laughed, he tried tickling me back as I tried to dodge, I saw myself in the air being spun. Shaye had carried me and spun me. I screamed with excitement, then he stopped. We looked deeply into each other's eyes and smiled. Then Shaye said

"That's why I love you, you always have your way of making me happy. I don't want to lose you never!"

"I love you too Shaye," I responded and we hugged each other.

9

Irene My Compulsory Twin

While we gazed into each other's eyes for a few seconds, which I thought would be our first kiss, the moment was interrupted by a familiar voice.

"Haba! Mr & Mrs! You are outside now! Get a room abeg and stop corrupting innocent eyes," Irene called out from inside the Cafeteria. Apparently, she had been watching us from the window.

Irene Okegbola was one of my course mates, her native name was Omowumi but she preferred to use her English name. She did not look like she was from the Western part of Nigeria, she looked more like she was from the Eastern part of Nigeria. She decided to maintain Irene so she would be unpredictable for her race. We were birthday mates, age mates and were of the same height. We went to the same primary and secondary school. She was a beautiful, shapely girl too, nominated for Miss Shape in secondary school, two-time punctuality prefect, best debater of our set and best behaved student. She was well-disciplined and I really liked and admired her. I was so glad to see her again when we ended up in the same University.

Irene was a born again Christian and always preached to me. I always told her I'd be her number one church member anytime she was ready to start her church but I wasn't ready to live a "caged" life like hers because I was already in one which was my home. At least that was how I viewed Christianity then.

"Oops. We forgot," Shaye said as he put me down. "We did not know we were already in front of the cafeteria."

"Hello my lovely Pastor Irene," I greeted Irene as Shaye and I entered the cafeteria.

She stood up to come greet us. Then, she tapped my shoulder in a girlish manner and said "Nawa for you o! No call, no text, no flash, no..."

"You, did you call? After all, I flashed you a few times," I interrupted.

Irene tried to defend herself but I immediately I replied, "You see! I better pass you, at least I flashed..."

"Flash, and you are proud to say it, imagine?" Irene said and we both laughed.

Flash is another expression in Nigeria of calling a person deliberately with the intention for the phone to ring but not for the person to pick up the call.

"May we sit down?" Shaye said reminding us that we were standing.

"Oh! Sorry Oga," Irene said, when she realised we had all being standing. Then we chose one of the tables at the corner of the cafeteria.

"Irene where were you posted?" I asked. "My dear, it's Lagos o!" She replied.

"Wow! This is good, I'm loving this!" I said, obviously excited.

Irene was surprised, "Shuu? Why?"

"I was also posted to Lagos!" I told her happily!

"Wow! That's great, we bless God, which means we will be together!" She said in her 'spirikoko' way.

"Perfectment!" I replied. "Perfectment!" is the French word for perfect.

"Spirikoko" is yet another expression used in Nigeria for Born Again Christians who are 100% devoted to their service and dedication to God. This is usually reflected in their conduct and conversations with people.

I was glad to have Irene posted to Lagos. At least, I'd have a familiar face with me in Lagos. I was definitely going to miss my dear Annabel but we would talk on phone and visit each other. Sometimes I wondered why Irene and I had to be together for so long; same primary school, same secondary school, same University now we were going to serve at the same place.

Shaye smiled and said, "That's beautiful at least I have someone to leave my baby with."

"Shaye where were you posted to?" Irene asked.

"PH." Shaye responded sharply.

"Wow, this is good. Thank God, Don't worry, God will see you through." Irene said as she looked at Shaye and I.

"Yes o! It's just that I'll miss my baby, it's inevitable," Shaye replied and looked at me. "The will of God has to be done!" He added.

"Don't worry, this will strengthen our love." I quickly interrupted before he made me go emotional.

"I believe distance should strengthen our love because we will miss each other but value ourselves more as long as we keep the communication active and also find time to visit each other." I said.

"Ok guys, I have to go now," Irene said as she picked her bag, "I have eaten already."

"Thanks Irene," Shaye and I chorused.

"See you at the camp." I said to her.

There was a long pause after Irene left, then, Shaye spoke up. "I'll miss you Derin but don't worry, I'll be faithful to you, I promise," he said as he placed his right palm on my cheek gently.

I rested my face in his palm and held his hand tightly to my cheek and said,

"Me too Shaye."

After the emotional moment, we shared our plans with each other after which, we ate and left for our various houses.

It was a long silent walk to the gate. It was getting

dark and the number of students had drastically reduced. The street of the school premises had become quiet and the breeze was cooler than it was earlier. We strolled to the gate together and took a bus home.

10

Back To Jos

While we were in the bus, Shaye affirmed his promise to stay faithful and promised to marry me after our NYSC. I found myself crying. Three weeks was like three years for someone whom we saw almost everyday. I loved Shaye but I was puzzled about the thought of marriage. I wanted to explore.

Shaye and I alighted at the last bus stop to my house, we hugged each other tightly and bade ourselves farewell. By this time, my tears had dried up and I walked home happily.

As I walked home happily, I reflected on what happened earlier that day. Home, as at then, was still my Aunty's house at Osun State.

My Aunty was staying alone as, her husband, who worked in Warri, came home only three to four times a year; her four children were all grown and were in different Universities, so she was glad to have company. The memory of Monday morning when I arrived her house still lingered. I was too excited to eat. We gisted all morning, so in the afternoon she presented me with a well prepared home made pounded yam with vegetable soup. The vegetable soup had in it assorted meat and fish. I enjoyed the meal with much relish and stayed up for a while catching up on things with my Aunty, as I waited for the food to digest. It was after the food digested I went to bed which was still early enough for me to prepare and also get enough rest before the morning after which was the day I was in school for my letter.

My Aunty was happy I was posted to Lagos. She told me, it would be an opportunity for me to be exposed. She said my parents may not like the idea but I should remain fearless and persuade them to allow me. She did not know what I had in mind. After our discussion, she gave me some tubers of yam and some other foodstuff to take along with me for my parents when I left the following day. After arranging the gifts beside my luggage, we both went to bed. I took the first bus to Jos the next morning.

During the journey to Jos, I remembered home in Jos and my countenance fell at the thought of my parents.

"I wonder what mum and dad will say about this now."

That thought burst the bubble of my excitement as it dawned on me that they may not like the idea of Lagos.

"Yes, I would miss them but will they allow me out

of their sight?" I asked myself.

"Mum may want to raise an eye brow about Lagos, she knew my tendency of wanting freedom. Daddy, on the other hand, may be okay with it but he would want me to live with one of his brothers or sisters or one of mum's relations." The conversation in my heart continued.

I did not want to live with any body. I wanted to stay on my own. Living with any relative was the same as living with my parents, I would be monitored. Yet if I did not agree to stay with any relations, it would look like I was rebellious. I'd have to choose between redeploying to Jos or going to Lagos to live with a relation.

After thinking hard about it, I was resolute to go to Lagos and not to stay with any relations. I heaved a deep sigh.

"I will sort myself out" I said to myself. I shook the worry out of my mind and enjoyed the rest of my journey to Jos.

I got to Jos at 8pm and took a cab home. The bus station to my house was one and a half hours without traffic. I got home at 9:30pm and knocked on the gate.

"Na who be that?" Musa our security guard called out asking who was at the gate as he opened the gate's slut to peep to see who was there.

"Na me Mallam" I answered back.

"Ha, Yarinya Derin, sannu dazuwa, Yaya tafiya? You bring something come for me?" He greeted me as he opened the pedestrian gate for me.

All he said in Hausa Language was "little Derin, welcome, How was your journey? Did you bring anything for me?"

Musa is fond of calling me "little" because he was employed when I was a toddler. I got accustomed to it over time. Hausa Language is the Language spoken in Northern Nigeria.

"Yawwa, Nagode, su iyayena na gida?" I responded that my day was fine and asked if my parents were home. He told me they were home.

As I walked towards the entrance door of the house, I braced up myself and adjusted my countenance. I told myself whatever mum and dad would do, I was determined to go serve in Lagos even if I had to leave the house without their consent. I was prepared to fight, I was set to stand up for myself, no more mummy and daddy's rule. I was ready to be a rebel.

11

House Arrest!

When I entered the house that evening, I met my mother in the sitting room watching TV. The sitting room in our home was moderately big. It had pictures of my parents and I. It started from when my parents got married, to when I was born, to when I was six month's old, to one year, five years, ten years, eighteen years, my matriculation and graduation ceremonies. A visitor needed not to be told about my family, the pictures told the story.

At the corners of the sitting room, there were flowers at both sides for decoration. We had a plant in our compound named Queen of the Night, the flowers of the plant had a lovely scent, so some stems were usually cut out at night, put in the sitting room and thrown away in the morning because the freshness would have been used up over the night.

"Good Evening ma," I knelt down completely to

greet my mum.

"Aderinmola, Ayaaba, Omo Ekun, Sannu, how are you and how was trip? How's your aunty? And your cousins? Hope they are all well?"

That's was my mother's way of responding to my greeting. She bombarded me with many questions leaving me to pick the one to answer first. She always believed one day I would be the wife of a king, hence she called me "Ayaaba" meaning the king's wife. "Omo Ekun" in Yoruba language, the language spoken in the western part of Nigeria means the child of a Tiger. Even though the Lion is believed to be the King of the Animal Kingdom and respected for it's boldness. In some circles, the Tiger is believed to be the strongest. Tiger, in this case, was a figurative expression of describing the strength of my Father. My mother always alluded to my ancestry which was a fierce one.

"Very fine, thank you ma, everyone is fine and they send their greetings. Aunty said I should give you these yam tubers and other foodstuff. She also gave me some money for transport." I showed my mum the bags of yam and other foodstuff.

"I trust my sister, she will never let you leave empty handed. Take the tubers to where we keep them and keep the money, after all it's yours," my mother said without even asking how much it was.

"Yes ma, Ina daddy?" I asked where my father was.

"He is in the bathroom. He will soon be out," My mother answered as she bent over to look out of the sitting room to confirm if my dad was out of the bathroom.

I told my mum where I had been posted to. My mum looked happy, but there was the flash of worry that passed through her face. I asked her what was wrong, "Lagos," she said as if she thought about it. "Lagos is too exposed for you."

I went close to her and tried to be patronising.

"Mum, don't worry, I'll be fine, some of my friends were posted there too."

"What of Annabel? Where was she posted to?" Mother asked.

"Zamfara," I responded.

"Hmm.." Mother sighed but I quickly interrupted her next statement.

"But Irene was posted to Lagos too. You remember Irene abi?" I asked.

At that point, my father came into the sitting room.

"Hey Baby, you are back, I didn't hear you come in. How was your trip?"

"Good evening Dad," I knelt down completely to greet my father

"Trip was fine, daddy," I answered excitedly. "I was posted to Lagos."

"No Way, I am going to call Toye now, he has to redeploy you to Jos." My father said without batting an eye lid.

Dad had met Mr. Toye barely two weeks ago through one of his trusted colleagues before I went to collect my call up letter. He had been recommended to my dad for a particular job that needed to be done in 24hours which he did well and my dad also paid him well. He was also connected to top NYSC officials. This my dad had discovered in the course of their conversation; my dad mentioned me to him but it was already late to work my posting to Jos, so he promised to do a redeployment to Jos for me when I'm posted out of Jos.

"No Daddy! Not again, I like Lagos, what profit will I be to you here in Jos as a corper? What is the essence of NYSC if I serve where I grew up, what is...?" I protested.

"Aderinmola Adeyosola, keep quiet! What right do you have to talk back when I'm talking. That is my decision and it is final," He replied.

At this point his voice was getting high. I looked at my mum expecting her to say something. My mum quietly turned her head away from me. I looked back at my father, the tears were welling up in my eyes. I was very angry. I felt like walking out of the sitting room but I remained glued to that spot.

I was shocked and puzzled at the switch in emotions in split seconds. I had never seen my father flip so fast. It felt like a movie and I had to pinch myself to be sure I was not dreaming. I had expected my mother to be the flippant one but to my utmost surprise, it was my father this time.

After a few seconds of awful silence, my mother spoke up calmly.

"Derin, take your things to the room, shower and rest from your trip. It's been a long day for you."

I gave my dad a second look, at that point, he had sat down already. He took the television remote and flipped through the channels while he also tried to pick his mobile phone beside him. I picked up my bag and walked angrily to the room. I fought back the tears determined to fight. I could feel fear creep in because I had never had a fall out with my parents before and once my father said "final" he meant it. I fell on my bed angry and sad at the same time, thinking of what to do.

12

Aunty Toke Rescued Me

I laid down on my bed speechless still thinking about what to do. A lot of thoughts swarm through my mind.

"Should I run away?" I asked myself.

"Maybe I should threaten to kill myself," I thought to myself.

"No, mummy and daddy will not give in to such threat, they are too strict and fearless, I will be flogged instead." The conversation continued.

From my room, I could hear my parents argue in the sitting room. I wasn't interested. I was too hurt and disappointed to know the outcome of their conversation.

"How will I convince them?" As I started slipping into thoughts again, my phone rang. It was Aunty

Toke, my mother's younger sister. She was the closest to me amongst all my Aunties. She always supported me. She was more than a sister to me.

"Hello Aunty," I picked the call, sadly.

"Omoge, how are you?" She asked in her warm way of greeting me. She called me "Omoge" most times which is a Yoruba way of calling "Fine girl" or "Finest"

"Aunty, I'm not fine. I went to collect my Call Up letter from school and I just got back to Jos from Ife tonight," I answered back.

"And so? Why are you sad? Where were you posted to?" She asked.

"Lagos," I answered.

"Ehen? You should be happy now? Is that not what you've always wanted?" She asked not too sure why I was sad.

"Aunty, I am, but mum and dad, especially dad..." my voice went quiet again.

"Uncle abi, what is he saying now?" She asked again.

"He wants his friend to redeploy me to Jos," I answered.

"Na wa o, this my sister's husband sef. Anyway, you are Daddy's girl, do you blame him?" She said.

"Aunty, I want to go to Lagos, I want to feel Lagos, I've heard so much about Lagos not to experience it, I..." I continued when she interrupted me.

"Ok dearie, I'll speak with them on your behalf,"

She said.

"Really?" My voice lightened up.

"Yes, really, now shey you will lighten up and give your Aunty Toke gist of your trip."

I excitedly gave her the gist of the trip, my friends at school and all that happened. We spoke for a long time and she warned me to be well behaved. She said she offered to speak with them on my behalf to give me a chance to grow on my own after many years of my parents' watchful eyes. I also told her to help me convince them not to let me live with any relative. At first she hesitated, then, she agreed on the condition that I would be of good behaviour and I would not disappoint her. I was grateful for what she was about to do for me so I thanked her and made her loads of promises but I had my plans.

13

Lagos! Here I Come!

The next morning I woke up still very angry even though I was half excited Aunty Toke would speak for me. I did not leave my room for most part of the morning. I silently hoped Aunty Toke would succeed in convincing my Father. Sometimes, it was my mother that needed the convincing but that time, it was my father. My father's reaction still baffled me. I thought he would be understanding but I was wrong. Half way through the day, I eventually stepped out of the room to have my bath. It must have taken me ages but when I finished, I got dressed and went to the kitchen to feed the worms calling for food in my stomach.

As I was grabbing the bottle of groundnut to keep my mouth busy, I noticed my mum had dozed off on the sofa in the sitting room on my father's laps. I could hear my dad speaking with someone on the phone, so I went to greet him. He answered me with a wave since he was on the phone. I could tell he was speaking with Aunty Toke. I walked back to the Kitchen to make my lunch while eavesdropping on their conversation.

"Look T, there is nothing anyone will tell me that I'll accept. Not even you. Derin is my only child, a girl for that matter. She has lived all her life in Jos except for when she went to Ife for her University, which I agreed to because of her mother's other sister, your eldest sister that is there to be checking up on her for us. And you know, If not for the intensity of her school work, I would have preferred she stayed off Campus." I heard my dad say to Aunty Toke. Of course, I could not hear Aunty Toke's response. Then again, I heard my dad respond.

"Toke, listen to me. Derin is going to be twenty years in December, what does she know? I don't want all those Lagos boys to take advantage of my child. No way! You say I'm overprotective, why won't I be? Do you know how long it took her Mother and I to have her? Have you forgotten the Doctor said we should not attempt having other children after two miscarriages my wife had else I'll lose my wife? How do you expect us to start over if anything happens to Derin?" My father protested further. Then, there was a pause and my father said again

"Olatoke, hmmm, you are saying I should let this girl go? Who will watch over her for me in Lagos?" My father asked.

After a long pause, I heard my father say "Take care of yourself Toke, I'll speak to you later."

My Jaw dropped as he ended the call. I felt like going to the sitting room and exploding on him but I just could not. The anger in me had built so much and was ready to erupt like a volcano. I wondered why my father was so adamant.

Aunty Toke was one of my Father's favourites among my mum's sisters. He called her the sister he never had. The bond between them was so strong that even my mother had to come to accept that after her and I, Aunty Toke was the next most important person in my father's life and this was because Aunty Toke had always supported the family through thick and thin from when my father and my mother met till date.

I was so angry, I could not cook again, I just turned off the cooker and stormed out of the kitchen straight to my room. I sensed that my father saw me but he acted like nothing happened. I slammed the door to my room, took the nearest object to me which was a tail comb and broke it in anger. I was breathing fast with bottled anger.

My phone rang, I saw it was Shaye calling, I ignored the call, I picked up my small mirror as a replacement for my phone and crushed it in between my palms. I could see blood. The mirror had cut my right palm. I was bleeding. I watched the blood drip. It was then I came to my senses and applied pressure to the injury. At this time, I started to cry.

"Whether Daddy likes it or not, I will go to Lagos," I reassured myself amidst the tears, cleaned my tears with the back of my hand while I kept applying pressure to the injury to stop the blood.

I was in my room for the rest of the day. I cried profusely, said nothing to anyone and none of my parents came to check me in the room. I understood why my mother could not come to check me. There was little she could say or do since my father insisted on redeployment. Most part of her supported my father's decision but the remaining part of her also understood that I could not be with them forever. The best she could do for my dad and I was to remain neutral and allowed us settle our differences ourselves.

After a few minutes, the blood stopped. I sat there on the floor of my room, numb and depressed for the rest of the day. I completely lost my appetite for food that day and I ended up sleeping on the floor of my room that night.

The next morning, which was a Friday morning, I was awoken as early as 6am with severe hunger pangs and headache. It was then I remembered I had not eaten for a whole day. I dragged myself up with my right hand on my forehead and my left hand on my stomach. I still felt a little pain on my right palm from the injury I inflicted on myself the previous day. The wound had become a scab. I applied methylated spirit on it, it hurt a little but I felt better afterwards.

My head felt like a trailer was dropping building blocks on it. My stomach felt it was been eaten up by termites. I went to the kitchen to get myself some bread and tea. While I was eating in the dinning room, my father came in.

"Ina Kwana Papa," I knelt down to say good morning to him, with no enthusiasm, stood up almost immediately and continued eating.

"Good Morning Derin," he answered back ignoring my indifferent greeting.

"When are you supposed to report at the Camp?" He asked.

"15th sir," I responded still not looking at him.

"That's next week Tuesday. Right?"

"Yes sir," I answered.

"Ok, preparation starts tomorrow. I have decided to let you go to your desired Lagos," He said in a lighter tone.

"Sir?" I looked up in amazement. The bread I was eating dropped into the plate. I thought I did not hear him clearly.

"B-bbut, I thought..." I was going to ask him about Mr. Toye he was going to call when he interrupted me.

"I said I have decided to let you go to your desired Lagos or don't you want to go again?" He asked when he saw the shock on my face.

My dull and angry face immediately melted into a warm smile. Then my dad continued

"Now, before you get too excited, make sure you say thank you to your mother and Aunty Toke. I'm sure you told Toke because you know she could get away with me after your mother, ba?" He asked with a questioning playful look he usually gave me when I was mischievous.

I only looked at him in amazement, I could not say a word but inside me, my thoughts screamed "Yes!" I almost jumped out of my body with excitement but I still didn't express it fully.

LAGOS! HERE I COME!

"Thank you daddy, you won't regret this, I promise! I promise!" I left my food to hug and peck him. He hugged me back and laughed. I was so happy, I ran to my mother who was just coming out of their room, thanked her graciously after greeting her.

I ran to my room with much excitement, called Aunty Toke, thanked her and reaffirmed my promises to her. She was glad she could help. I heard my father's voice from a distance, the conversation sounded like he was speaking with Aunty Toke. She must have called my dad to thank him for listening to her. After a short time, she called me back to let me know she had called my dad and gave me a final warning not to disappoint her. I ended the call, pinched myself to be sure I was not dreaming. By this time, the headache and hunger pangs had disappeared mysteriously. I was too excited to remember there was something wrong with me when I woke up.

I shut the door of my room and jumped with joy as I looked into my dressing mirror and said to myself "Yes! Yes! Yes! Finally baby girl it's time for you explore and express yourself! Express yourself Now! Now!" I sang the legend advert tune. I did a 360 turn and almost screamed when I remembered I was still home so I kept quiet. I fell backwards on my bed and heaved a deep sigh of relief. I called Shaye back to apologise for not picking his call the previous day. I explained to him what happened and he was happy, I was finally allowed to go and serve in Lagos. We ended our conversation and I knew I was set for a new chapter of my life.

The remaining days were busy with preparations. I got more calls from family and friends. I shopped happily with my mum as I strategized and planned the next three weeks at the orientation camp in my head. I eagerly looked forward to 15th October, which was just less than five days away.

The night before the trip, Shaye and I spoke on the phone. We talked all through the night till the next morning until it was time for him to go and prepare for the trip. I cried a little after we finished talking before I slept off around 4am. I had barely slept deeply before my father knocked on my door at 4:30am.

Once it was 5:15am, we left the house for the airport. It was still a little dark outside but there were cars already on the streets as people were on their way to their various offices because it was a working day. My mum had made me some egg on toast to take along in case there was no time to eat at home. It was my first time travelling by air so my mum gave me lots of health safety tips.

"If only she knew her daughter was not aero phobic she would not say all these," I thought to myself as I listened to her and noted the tips.

We got to the airport at 6:00am on the dot. Immediately, I joined the check-in line and in 15 mins I was ready to leave for the departure lounge. I hugged my parents and bade them farewell. I felt like flying literally but I still had to wait for the next 45mins. Shaye was going by road and he had left very early.

"Attention please, Aero Contractors AJ124 going to Lagos is ready to board, passengers should please come on board. Thank you" the female voice announced at 7am. Immediately, I joined the queue and we all boarded. I sat beside the window because I wanted to see how the pillows of cloud looked like at closer view. At 7:50am, the plane was ready to take off.

While the usual safety precautions were given, I sent a text to my parents, friends and Shaye, then I switched off my phone. As the plane sped through the runway, ready to fly, I smiled to myself and said quietly and happily "Lagos, wait for me, Aderinmola Adeyosola is coming in grand style!" The plane took off into the air in a glamorous eagle like manner and settled comfortably in the sky heading for Lagos.

14

Epilogue

I wanted freedom and nothing but freedom. I had been closed or caged for long. Or so, I thought. I felt, I did not live life to the fullest. Yes, NYSC came. That moment of freedom came and I was desperate to let it all out. Travelling down to Lagos was a dream come true and yes, I was determined to explore.

I succeeded in getting across to Idunnu Aina. She was excited to hear from me. She told me she was a fan and felt honoured to be called by me. She was however disappointed when she heard her parents gave me her contact. She was upset with them but was willing to hear me out. I fixed an appointment with her and her parents for the next week. Idunnu was elated. She was delighted to come and hoped I could help convince her parents to grant her her freedom. I also called her parents back. They were glad at the news that their daughter was willing to meet with me. I suggested they came over with her and they obliged.

The appointment was August 10 for 12pm. The Aina family were there an hour ahead but I had a client and they did not mind waiting. When I was through with my client at exactly 12pm, I requested for them and the family of three walked in into my office.

"Thank you for coming, please have your seat," I said to the family of three.

"It's great to finally meet you Idunnu," I said to their daughter.

"The honour is mine ma," The obviously excited young girl replied.

She came close not minding the presence of her parents and asked,"could I hug you ma?"

"Oh yes, come," I went closer and hugged her.

She held me tightly for a few more seconds. I could feel the crave for love, attention and understanding in her hug, so I stayed till she loosened her grip. My eyes were shut all through, I wanted to help Idunnu so much and I was willing to give it my best shot. After what seemed to look like forever, she let go.

"Thank you ma, I needed that so bad," She said.

"I know, you are welcome dear," I replied.

Mr & Mrs Aina only watched the drama quietly waiting for what was about to transpire. I went back to my seat to sit down, just as Idunnu did same.

"I have listened to your parents Idunnu and I know I haven't heard your side of the story. Just as agreed,

I have invited you and your parents at the same time to express your grievances to them in a respectful yet truthful way and they are willing to listen. So, we are all ears."

"Yes ma, thank you ma," She started.

"First, I'd like to apologise to my parents for being rude to them and misbehaving but I have my reasons..."She continued.

Idunnu narrated to us why she was not happy at home, she said there were so many rules at home, she was not allowed to discuss matters of the heart and sex matters at home, she had peer concerns she wanted to talk about but could not and movies were censored because of her. Her friends enjoyed themselves and could travel anywhere they wanted. Her only opportunity of living outside home and to experience life herself was to stay on campus. All she asked for was to spend her final year on campus but her parents had refused. She had been practically begging them for three years of her life but they had refused. The last time, it was agreed that when she got to her final year, she would be allowed to but to her utmost surprise, when she got to her final year the story changed, so she decided to rebel.

I listened to every detail of her story with rapt attention. The story sounded similar to mine and I could identify with her. When she was through, I looked at her parents. I could see the shock on their faces. At this point, there was a disturbing silence in the room. One could hear a pin drop because of the level of silence in the room. We all kept mute as we thought about what Idunnu just narrated.

COMING SOON...

DIAMOND IN THE ROUGH

PLATOON II

BOOK TWO

ADEBOLA A. AYOADE